This Orchard
book belongs to

....

....

....

For the new generation, Maya and Dylan – A.M.

For Isabel, a sweet little pea – P.D.

ORCHARD BOOKS
338 Euston Road, London NW1 3BH

Orchard Books Australia
Level 17/207, Kent Street, Sydney, NSW 2000

First published in 2010 by Orchard Books
First published in paperback in 2011

Text © Allan Manham 2010
Illustrations © Penny Dann 2010

The rights of Allan Manham to be identified as the author and of
Penny Dann to be identified as the illustrator of this work have been asserted by them
in accordance with the Copyright, Designs and Patents Act, 1988.

A CIP catalogue record for this book is available from the British Library.

ISBN 978 1 84362 592 6

1 3 5 7 9 10 8 6 4 2

Printed in China

Orchard Books is a division of Hachette Children's Books,
an Hachette UK company.

www.hachette.co.uk

THE GIANT CARROT

Planted by
Allan Manham

SWEDE
DREAMS
by
DOUG
McArrot

Grown by
Penny Dann

ORCHARD BOOKS

Jack was an excellent gardener.

Every morning he got on his bicycle

and went to see how his vegetables were growing.

Jack grew more vegetables than all the other gardeners, and his were always the biggest and the best.

Every day, Jack
dug and dug
and raked and raked . . .

and watered
and watered.
And every day his vegetables
grew
and
grew.

Jack was particularly proud
of his carrots.

One day, he was just in the mood
for a bowl of hot carrot soup.

So, bending down,
he tugged at the top
of the biggest carrot.
BUT IT
WOULDN'T
BUDGE!

So he pulled
and he pulled . . .

But still the carrot
WOULDN'T BUDGE!

Jack called to Bertha
to give him a hand.

They **pulled**

and they **pulled**....

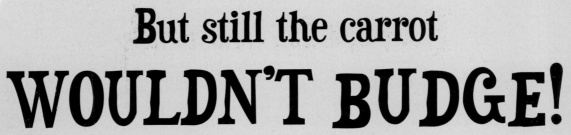

But still the carrot
WOULDN'T BUDGE!

Betty and **B**ob came to help.

Bob and Betty and Bertha and Jack
all pulled on the carrot.
They pulled and they pulled . . .

But still the carrot
WOULDN'T BUDGE!

Then Jake
joined in.

And Phoebe
helped too.

Phoebe and Jake and Bob and Betty and Bertha and Jack
all pulled on the carrot.

They pulled and they pulled . . .

But still the carrot

WOULDN'T BUDGE!

Charlie decided
to have a go.

And Henry
came too.

Charlie and Henry and Phoebe and Jake and Bob and Betty and Bertha and Jack all pulled on the carrot.

They pulled and they pulled . . .

But that carrot was Stuck!

All the pulling and pulling
was starting to stir up dust.

And the dust began to tickle Jack's nose...

Ah ... Ahh ...

With that, the giant carrot
shot right out of the ground!

And they all fell backwards . . .

. . . in a giant

HEAP!

Jack was
very pleased!

The carrot was **SO** big

he was able to make hot soup for . . .

every

one!